THE EYE OF ARGON

THE EYE OF ARGON

JIM THEIS

WILDSIDE PRESS

THE EYE OF ARGON

Copyright © 2006 by **Wildside Press, LLC.**

Introduction copyright © 2006 by **Lee Weinstein.**

Wildside Press
www.wildsidepress.com

IN SEARCH OF JIM THEIS

LEE WEINSTEIN

"The weather beaten trail wound ahead into the dust racked climes of the baren land which dominates large portions of the Norgolian empire."

Thus begins the tale, "The Eye of Argon," (TEoA) which has become a hilarious staple of science fiction convention programming over the last several decades. Most regular attendees of conventions have at one time or another come across the program item known as the "Eye of Argon" reading. People sit in a circle and take turns reading from photocopies of the story. The reader's turn is over when he begins to laugh uncontrollably.

"The Eye of Argon," with its malapropisms, typos and inimitable turns of phrase has earned a reputation as the apotheosis of bad writing.

The story itself, a 7000-word novelette, is a sword-and-sorcery adventure featuring a Conanesque barbarian named Grignr who attempts to get the titular jewel, the eye of an idol. The story ended abruptly as Grignr is about to be engulfed by bubbling ooze.

The story is purported to be a naive work by an inexperienced would-be writer. But rumors have circulated to the present day that the story was written as a deliberate send-up by a professional. It is easy to see why. The word choices and mistakes seem to be just a bit too much over the top.

"Grignr's emerald green orbs glared lustfully at the wallowing soldier struggling before his chestnut swirled mount."

"Gaping from its single obling socket was scintillating, many fauceted scarlet emerald, a brilliant gem seeming to possess a life all its own."

"Aye. My people are not tarnished by petty luxuries and baubles."

The sentences often sound like they were constructed like the "Mad-Libs" game from *Mad Magazine* where the author fills in the blanks with the most inappropriate word choices possible.

The story of the origin of "The Eye of Argon," which I first heard in the late 70's, had always struck me as a bit questionable. I had originally heard, years ago, that Dorothy Fontana, of Star Trek fame, had come across a mimeographed fanzine containing the story, and found it so unintentionally funny that she felt compelled to retype it and distribute photocopies to her friends. It gradually spread through fandom by photocopies and word of mouth, the original source being lost and forgotten in the process.

I always wondered why she would have retyped it rather than making a photocopy. It also seemed a little suspicious that the original fanzine was not cited in the copies. There was simply the title and the author's name, Jim Theis. It was possible that the fanzine was badly printed and therefore difficult to copy, and she may have simply not bothered to cite the source, but it all sounded a little too convenient as an explanation for TEoA's origin.

Furthermore, in later years I heard other versions of the story. In one, the fanzine had been found by the late author, Thomas Scortia. He had given it to Chelsea Quinn Yarbro and she had retyped it. According to another version of the story, current on the internet, the manuscript had simply been found abandoned at on a table at a convention. The existence of various versions of the origin story coupled with the lack of any sort of documentation seemed to lend credence to the persistent rumors it had been deliberately written by a pro.

In 1987, the story saw its first formal publication. Hypatia Press in Eugene, Oregon, reprinted the story as a pamphlet. The cover proclaimed the pamphlet as number one in the "Socialogical [sic] Explorations" series. This was complete with chapter titles (the passed-around photocopies merely had chapter numbers), and illustrations by Lynne Adams. Suspiciously, there was no information concerning the supposed original fanzine printing. Darrell Schweitzer told me he had received from Alan Newcomer of Hypatia Press, around this time, a photocopy which was supposed to have been reproduced from the original fanzine, including some artwork. I examined it, and strangely, there was again no citation for the mysterious fanzine.

Also in 1987, possibly inspired by the above pamphlet, Schweitzer wrote an article on the subject, which appeared in *Fantasy Review,* entitled "One Fine Day in the Stygian Haunts of Hell: Being the Lore and Legend of the Fabled 'The Eye of Argon.'"

Schweitzer's article outlines the origins of the story as being retyped by an unidentified pro who got a fanzine from Thomas Scortia, notes the existence of variant texts circulating throughout fandom, and mentions the rumors of the story having been written by a professional. He also mentions rumors of the author having been found, still believing that his story was a good one. At the end of the article, Schweitzer asks that the real Jim Theis come forward and identify himself. When the essay was reprinted in Schweitzer's essay collection, *Windows of the Imagination* in 1997, he adds a note that he received no feedback from the publication of the essay, because there were no further issues of *Fantasy Review.* He also adds a 1997 update in which he says a reprint of the essay, which appeared in a fanzine, drew no response and that "urban legends" about Theis continued to circulate around fandom.

I strongly suspected that there was no fanzine, and that

someone, possibly a professional, had concocted the story as a hoax, and that the various versions of who had found the story were folklore.

That changed when toward the end of October, 2002, I received an email, forwarded by a friend. The email claimed that the author of TEoA, Jim Theis, had been found. A little startled, I decided to find out once and for all where TEoA had come from.

The email I had received contained a link to the website of a British fan named Susan Stepney. Stepney had quite a tribute to the story on her website, including various versions that had been translated into foreign languages and back again.

She also mentioned that Jim Theis had been interviewed on an SF related radio talk show in Los Angeles called Hour 25. The catch was, the interview had taken place in 1984. But she said she had heard tapes of the interview.

According to Stepney, Theis had written the story when he was about sixteen. She also noted that he had gone on to be a writer and that there were other stories about Grignr.

I wondered how it was possible that the author of the infamous "Eye of Argon" had appeared on the radio in Los Angeles where he must have been heard by at least several hundred fans, and yet news of this was only now surfacing?

When I read it through more thoroughly, though, I found the statement that the interview might not actually have aired.

About a year or so earlier, I had scanned the internet for

information on Theis and *The Eye of Argon* and found nothing but postings of the story itself.

Now I was curious. Had there really been such an interview? I found a website for the radio show and contacted the archivist by email.

Then I followed some links and discovered an interesting quote attributed to author Stephen Goldin. Goldin was quoted as saying that during a convention he had met a woman who told him she had turned the crank on the mimeo for the Ozark-area fanzine that contained the story.

This was interesting. The fanzine was still unnamed, but now I knew that it was supposed to have been in the Ozark area.

Nonetheless, there was no solid information. Just that an unnamed woman at an unnamed convention had helped to crank out an unnamed fanzine.

In searching about the web I found a website called Wulf's "Eye of Argon" Shrine. The webmaster made the statement that for all the horrible writing, the story was actually well paced and plotted. He went on to say that, although he didn't believe it himself, "at least one SF professional today claims that the story was a cunning piece of satire passed off as real fan fiction."

There seemed to be little else on the web, aside from endless repostings of the story itself, one of which was done up as a Mystery Science Theater 3000 pastiche. I decided to contact Stephen Goldin. But first, I turned my attention to the Usenet groups.

And here I began to hit pay dirt. First I found a rumor

that in the original fanzine, the story had appeared with illustrations by the author.

Then I found a question posted to the alt.sf lovers group asking if *The Eye of Argon* had been a deliberate attempt at a joke or was really an honest amateurish effort. The asker suspected the former because he believed one had to know what one was doing to write something so consistently funny. He also noted that no serious writer would use headings like "chapter 3 ½" or make reference to a "red emerald."

There were two replies to his question. One was from a fan, who claimed to have seen the original mimeo and said he knew the people who had transcribed it into electronic format. However, he provided no solid information.

But the second response was from a fan named Rich Zellich who was involved in running Archon, the St. Louis regional convention. Since Archon is run by the Ozark Science Fiction Association, or its current descendant, this seemed to corroborate what Goldin had been told. Zellich said that not only was Jim Theis real, but that he was a regular attendee at the convention.

This was indeed news. I was about to email Mr. Zellich when I noticed the date on all three postings. They were all from 1991. This was old news. I would have to find out if Zellich was still at the same address. Somehow, it seemed, the mysterious Mr. Theis was still a regular con-goer a decade ago and yet was unknown to the rest of fandom, except as a byline on a widely circulated story, even now, over a decade later.

I found the website for Archon, and discovered they had conveniently archived lists of guests for years past. I went back to the list for 1996, and sure enough, there was a Jim Theis listed.

I decided to look further on the newsgroups. I then came up with a posting from 1994 from a Richard Newsome. And here was the smoking gun. Here was the critical piece of information. According to Newsome, the story had originally appeared in a fanzine called *Osfan*, in issue 10. Here was the long missing citation. It was beginning to look as if the dubious-sounding origin story of "Eye" had a kernel of truth to it after all.

Newsome followed this information up in another posting which contained a transcription of an interview with Theis published in *Osfan* 13 a few months later.

This is most of the interview as posted, with some material about local fan politics deleted:

OSFAN: What did you think of your story "Eye of Argon" in *Osfan* 10?

THEIS: I admit I did make a few mistakes. But then, I'm just sixteen-years-old. The editing that was done to it did not help it. In the future, if I have anything published I would appreciate it if it were published as it was written.

OSFAN: Is there anything in "Eye of Argon" that you would have changed now that you have re-read it in *Osfan* 10?

THEIS: In fact, I have changed it. I went over it for an independent study for English in school. You know, like adjectives changed and places where sentences should be deleted; things of this type. Even so it is nothing to be proud of and yet it is. Because how many people have had their first story published at sixteen — even if it is in a fanzine or a club-zine? How many professional writers have written a complete story at so early an age? Even so, "Eye of Argon" isn't great. I basically don't know much about structure or composition.

OSFAN: Are you now working on structure, composition and grammar?

THEIS: Yes I am but it is difficult because I'm still in high school and must work on my writing in my spare time. Basically, these books on English composition haven't taught me anything I didn't know but they are showing me how to put them (composition, grammar, etc.) into a working order.

OSFAN: I am personally proud of your story for *Osfan* 10, in the sense that it is more than I could have done. Also, the fact that when they were kidding you about it, you took it so well. I think you should be given a pat on the back for such good sportsmanship. You showed real character.

THEIS: I didn't know that. I mean, it was easier than showing bad character and inviting trouble.

Was this interview genuine? Or was it part of an elaborate put-on?

The ultimate answer would lie in *Osfan* 10 itself, if it indeed existed. Getting a hold of a possibly-obscure thirty year-old fanzine might have proved to be a problem. But Temple University in Philadelphia houses the David Paskow Collection, a science fiction research collection which includes an enormous selection of fanzines. I checked their catalogue, and happily, they owned a copy of *Osfan* 10.

Meanwhile I received a reply from the archivist at the radio station. He essentially confirmed that he did have the interview somewhere, but he couldn't put his hands on it at the moment, and that he wasn't sure if he'd be posting it. But it was now a moot point.

I went to the Temple campus at the first available opportunity.

Osfan was the official fanzine of the Ozark Science Fiction Association and came out on a more or less monthly basis.

Osfan 10 is a mimeographed fanzine, the cover of which has a drawing of something that looks like a cross between an alligator and Barney the Dinosaur. Above it, in imitation gothic-style letting, is the word "Ghod." Also on the cover are the words "The August 21st issue of the monthly publication of the Ozark Science Fiction Association." There was no year indicated anywhere, but according to the library catalog it was published in 1970. The postmark on it was dated 1971.

The contents are typical for a fanzine of the period.

There are con reports, poetry, fan art, and local gossip. But my attention was immediately drawn to the last item listed on the table of contents: "The Eye of Argon" (novelette) by Jim Theis.

And there it was. The rumor that it was illustrated by the author was not true. There were some spot illos interspersed in the text, but they were by different artists and were not connected to the story.

As for the missing page at the end, alas, it was still missing. In fact, there were at least two pages missing. The last page of the issue I held, page 46, leaves off as Grignr warns his companion to be quiet as they sneak through a tunnel. The bubbling ooze doesn't make its appearance until a couple of pages later.

I then took a look at Darrell Schweitzer's photocopy which was supposed to have come from the original fanzine. The copy included a handwritten note across the top of the front page, which read: "Dear Quinn – Here is a piece of FINE writing we can enjoy – Tom." Sure enough, it matched up, spot illo for spot illo with the *Osfan* text. The photocopy, however, went to page 4 and the bubbling ooze. The note seemed to confirm the story that it had been sent to Chelsea Quinn Yarbro from Thomas Scortia.

The issue also contained an article, by Jim Theis, giving an account of a party he had recently attended. Theis was an active fan at the time.

Meanwhile, while recounting my researching adventures to a friend, he told me that he had just been to an Archon about a month previously (2002). He told me that he had attended the "Eye of Argon" reading, and had heard an announcement there that Jim Theis had passed away.

I emailed Rich Zellich after all, and he confirmed the story. Theis had indeed passed away, although he didn't have any details.

He referred me to a friend of Theis's. I've emailed this person several times, but have never received a response.

But it was clear that Theis was a good sport about the whole thing, often attending the readings.

I later located his death notice in the *St. Louis Dispatch* for March 29, 2002. Elusive to the end, he had tragically passed away on March 26, 2002, leaving behind a wife and two sons.

In any case, it was now clear that TEoA was a sincere effort by a sixteen-year-old rather than a deliberate hoax. But there were a few questions remaining. There was still the matter of the variant versions of how the story came to be circulated in fandom.

This is what Chelsea Quinn Yarbro had to say in a personal communication of 9/9/03 to Darrell Schweitzer:

> Tom Scortia sent me the fanzine pages as a kind of shared amusement, since both of us tended to look for poor use of language in stories. Don Simpson and I were still married then, and one of our entertainments was reading aloud to each other. This work was such a mish-mash that we took turns reading it to each other until we could bear no more.
>
> About two weeks after the story arrived, we had a dinner party, mainly for MWA and book dealer friends, and Joe Gores got to talking about some of the

really hideous language misuse he had seen in recent anthology submissions, and had brought along a few of the most egregious. I mentioned I had something that put his examples in the shade, and brought out "The Eye of Argon." It was a huge hit. Tom Whitmore asked if he could make a copy of it, and I loaned it to him, and readings of it started to become a hideous entertainment. I never typed out a copy of it, but I am afraid I did start the ball rolling.

I contacted Stephen Goldin and asked about whether Dorothy Fontana had been involved. He sent the details in a personal communication of 9/9/03:

I first encountered *The Eye of Argon* while visiting Quinn's house, and loved it so much I imposed on her to make a copy for me, which I took back home to Los Angeles. I saw to it that the story got read on as many occasions as possible, and my copy was getting pretty tattered. One year, for my birthday, Dorothy Fontana lovingly retyped and bound a copy for me (a very difficult job, since she attempted to retain all the original typos.) That's how she came into the picture, but she by no means discovered it. The blame rests solely on Tom Scortia's shoulders.

These communications cleared up the confusion surrounding how the copies of the story had become generally spread around fandom. But I was left with another, more troublesome question. How was it possible that Mr. Theis and his story had begun to accrete layers of folklore and misinformation when in fact he had remained in fandom until quite recently?

There are other examples of such occurrances. For example, I have come across rumors circulating on Usenet groups that horror writer Thomas Ligotti does not exist. Some fans have theorized that Ligotti's stories are by another writer who is using the name Ligotti as a disguise.

This is undoubedly because Ligotti is a reclusive writer who never attends conventions or makes public appearances.

But Theis apparently remained active, attending local conventions and being interviewed on the radio.

But there is a more striking example outside of fandom. In the 1950's there was a popular pin-up model named Bettie (or sometimes Betty) Page. She appeared in all manner of men's magazines and nudie-cutie film loops. In 1957 she gave up her modeling career and suddenly dropped from sight. Her photos and films, however, steadily gained in popularity. Bettie became a cult figure of monumental proportions as the sixties segued into the seventies and eighties. There were Bettie posters, Bettie dolls, and Bettie magazines. But Bettie herself seemed to have dropped off the face of the earth.

Decades went by. Rumors circulated about her fate. Some thought she had been murdered. Others thought she had left the country. Periodically, there were Elvis-like Bettie sightings.

Then in 1992 a reporter managed to solve the mystery,

and traced her whereabouts through a brother. It seemed that in the late 1957 Bettie had moved to Florida, joined an evangelical church, and became a born-again Christian. All the while her image had been rising to cult status, she herself had been traveling around the country attending bible colleges, and doing missionary work. At one point she was in the Billy Graham Crusade. For about thirty-five years the Bettie Page cult phenomenon had spread while Bettie Page herself had criss-crossed the country, each unaware of the other.

When she was finally found and contacted in the early 1992, she was totally astounded (and actually pleased!) that she had become an icon.

However, while Bettie Page story is written on a canvas that covers the entire United States and involves two separate sub-cultures that have little overlap, the Jim Theis story takes place in the presumably single subculture of science fiction fandom.

This I will have to leave to sociologists to figure out.

As for Theis' intent in writing the story, I will again quote Stephen Goldin:

For years I heard debate about whether it was a deliberate parody or simply that bad. At a Westercon a few years ago I met a woman who'd known Jim Theis, and in fact turned the crank on the mimeo that printed the story. She said he was very earnest about it—and that there were more stories of Grignr the Ecordian!

Then there is the matter of the missing pages. It was unfortunate that the copy of *Osfan* 10 I found was missing even more than the standard circulating version, which ended on page 48 of *Osfan* 10 with the words, "The jelly like mass began to bubble like a vat of boiling tar as quivers passed up and down its entire form." Surely there are complete issues of this fanzine out there somewhere.

Finally, after my research was all said and done, an item was brought to my attention that appeared in *Ansible* 193. In it Dave Langford printed a report from Michael Swanwick saying:

> I had a surprising conversation at Readercon with literary superstar Samuel R. Delany, who told me of how at an early Clarion the students and teachers had decided to see exactly how bad a story they could write if they put their minds to it. Chip himself contributed a paragraph to the round robin effort. Its title? "The Eye of Argon."

I attempted to contact Mr. Delany by email, but received no response. Langford does add the note, however, that Delany was surely misremembering something. This is evidently the case.

I have no doubt that rumors will continue to circulate about sightings of Mr. Theis and the professional origins of the tale. During the TEoA reading at Philcon in December of 2003 I heard fans wondering aloud if the story was a hoax.

I originally ended the foregoing article with the following plea:

> " . . . if anyone, anywhere has a complete copy of *Osfan* 10, please speak up. Fandom is waiting to hear the exciting conclusion of 'The Eye of Argon!'"

That plea was soon to be answered.

Shortly after my article, appeared in *NYSFR*, I found a message on my answering machine. It was from a woman who identified herself as Melveta Walker of the Golden Library of the University of New Mexico. She wanted to know if I was the Lee Weinstein who had written the recent article in *The New York Review of Science Fiction* , and that if I were, would I please call them back and ask for Gene Bundy.

Curious, I called the number she had given me. Mr. Bundy was away for the Thankgiving holiday, but I was informed by the graduate student who answered that Gene Bundy was the special collections librarian at the University and was in charge of the Jack Williamson collection, which she explained was the third largest collection of science fiction material in the world. Mr. Bundy had wanted me to contact him because he had the missing final page of "The Eye of Argon!" and they were all quite excited about it. It was exciting news indeed, and the following Monday I spoke to Gene Bundy himself.

He told me they had just inventoried and re-housed their enormous collection of fanzines, and after reading my article, he had searched the collection and found a pristine copy of *Osfan* 10. The fanzine was bound with staples, and the final page had evidently been lost from most copies, but this particular copy, which had been owned by Jack Williamson, was intact. The library staff felt that finding the intact fanzine helped to justify the enormous amount of work put into maintaining the collection.

Mr. Bundy graciously sent me a photocopy of the missing final page which I have transcribed. It saw the light of day for the first time in thirty-four years at Philcon 2004 on Dec. 10th, when it was read aloud by the winner of the annual "Eye of Argon" reading at the end of the session.

At the end of the final page, following Theis's byline, are the words "winner of the Jay T. Rikosh award for excellence." Who Rikosh is or was or what the significance the award was I had no idea at the time. I have since discovered that Rikosh was an artist whose work appeared in *Osfan* and the award was supposed to be a humorous booby prize. Theis was the first recipient.

"The Eye of Argon," for better or worse, is now complete. Unless, of course, someone decides to find out if Jim Theis had really written further tales of the adventures of Grignr the Barbarian.

Lee Weinstein
Philadelphia

THE EYE OF ARGON

The weather beaten trail wound ahead into the dust racked climes of the baren land which dominates large portions of the Norgolian empire. Age worn hoof prints smothered by the sifting sands of time shone dully against the dust splattered crust of earth. The tireless sun cast its parching rays of incandescense from overhead, half way through its daily revolution. Small rodents scampered about, occupying themselves in the daily accomplishments of their dismal lives. Dust sprayed over three heaving mounts in blinding clouds, while they bore the burdonsome cargoes of their struggling overseers.

"Prepare to embrace your creators in the stygian haunts of hell, barbarian", gasped the first soldier.

"Only after you have kissed the fleeting stead of death, wretch!" returned Grignr.

A sweeping blade of flashing steel riveted from the massive barbarians hide enameled shield as his rippling right arm thrust forth, sending a steel shod blade to the hilt into the soldiers vital organs. The disemboweled mercenary crumpled from his saddle and sank to the clouded sward, sprinkling the parched dust with crimson droplets of escaping life fluid.

The enthused barbarian swilveled about, his shock of fiery red hair tossing robustly in the humid air currents as he faced the attack of the defeated soldier's fellow in arms.

"Damn you, barbarian" Shrieked the soldier as he observed his comrade in death.

A gleaming scimitar smote a heavy blow against the renegade's spiked helmet, bringing a heavy cloud over the Ecordian's misting brain. Shaking off the effects of the pounding blow to his head, Grignr brought down his scarlet streaked edge against the soldier's crudely forged hauberk, clanging harmlessly to the left side of his opponent. The soldier's stead whinnied as he directed the horse back from the driving blade of the barbarian. Grignr leashed his mount forward as the hoarsely piercing battle cry of his wilderness bred race resounded from his grinding lungs. A twirling blade bounced harmlessly from the mighty thief's buckler as his rolling right arm cleft upward, sending a foot of blinding steel ripping through the Simarian's exposed gullet. A gasping gurgle from the soldier's writhing mouth as he tumbled to the golden sand at his feet, and wormed agonizingly in his death bed.

Grignr's emerald green orbs glared lustfully at the wallowing soldier struggling before his chestnut swirled mount. His scowling voice reverberated over the dying form in a tone of mocking mirth. "You city bred dogs should learn not to antagonize your better." Reining his weary mount ahead, grignr resumed his journey to the Noregolian city of Gorzam, hoping to discover wine, women, and adventure to boil the wild blood coarsing through his savage veins.

The trek to Gorzom was forced upon Grignr when the soldiers of Crin were leashed upon him by a faithless concubine he had wooed. His scandalous activities throughout the Simarian city had unleashed throngs of havoc and uproar among it's refined patricians, leading them to tack a heavy reward over his head.

He had barely managed to escape through the back entrance of the inn he had been guzzling in, as a squad of soldiers tounced upon him. After spilling a spout of blood from the leader of the mercenaries as he dismembered one of the officer's arms, he retreated to his mount to make his way towards Gorzom, rumoured to contain hoards of plunder, and many young wenches for any man who has the backbone to wrest them away.

-2-

Arriving after dusk in Gorzom, grignr descended down a dismal alley, reining his horse before a beaten tavern. The redhaired giant strode into the dimly lit hostelry reeking of foul odors, and cheap wine. The air was heavy with chocking fumes spewing from smolderingtorches encased within theden's earthen packed walls. Tables were clustered with groups of drunken thieves, and cutthroats, tossing dice, or making love to willing prostitutes.

Eyeing a slender female crouched alone at a nearby bench, Grignr advanced wishing to wholesomely occupy his time. The flickering torches cast weird shafts of luminescence dancing over the half naked harlot of his choice, her stringy orchid twines of hair swaying gracefully over the lithe opaque nose, as she raised a half drained mug to her pale red lips.

Glancing upward, the alluring complexion noted the stalwart giant as he rapidly approached. A faint glimmer sparked from the pair of deep blue ovals of the amorous female as she motioned toward Grignr, enticing him to join her. The barbarian seated himself upon a stool at the wenches side, exposing his body, naked save for a loin cloth brandishing a long steel broad sword, an iron spiraled battle helmet, and a thick leather sandals, to her unobstructed view.

"Thou hast need to occupy your time, barbarian",questioned the female?

"Only if something worth offering is within my reach." Stated Grignr,as his hands crept to embrace the tempting female, who welcomed them with open willingness.

"From where do you come barbarian, and by what are you called?" Gasped the complying wench, as Grignr smothered her lips with the blazing touch of his flaming mouth.

The engrossed titan ignored the queries of the inquisitive female, pulling her towards him and crushing her sagging nipples to his yearning chest. Without struggle she gave in, winding her soft arms around the harshly bronzedhide of Grignr corded shoulder blades, as his calloused hands caressed her firm protruding busts.

"You make love well wench," Admitted Grignr as he reached for the vessel of potent wine his charge had been quaffing.

A flying foot caught the mug Grignr had taken hold of, sending its blood red contents sloshing over a flickering crescent; leashing tongues of bright orange flame to the foot trodden floor.

"Remove yourself Sirrah, the wench belongs to me;"

Blabbered a drunken soldier, too far consumed by the influences of his virile brew to take note of the superior size of his adversary.

Grignr lithly bounded from the startled female, his face lit up to an ashen red ferocity, and eyes locked in a searing feral blaze toward the swaying soldier.

"To hell with you, braggard!" Bellowed the angered Ecordian, as he hefted his finely honed broad sword.

The staggering soldier clumsily reached towards the pommel of his dangling sword, but before his hands ever touched the oaken hilt a silvered flash was slicing the heavy air. The thews of the savages lashing right arm bulged from the glistening bronzed hide as his blade bit deeply into the soldiers neck, loping off the confused head of his senseless tormentor.

With a nauseating thud the severed oval toppled to the floor, as the segregated torso of Grignr's bovine antagonist swayed, then collapsed in a pool of swirled crimson.

In the confusion the soldier's fellows confronted Grignr with unsheathed cutlasses, directed toward the latters scowling make-up.

"The slut should have picked his quarry more carefully!" Roared the victor in a mocking baritone growl, as he wiped his dripping blade on the prostrate form, and returned it to its scabbard.

"The fool should have shown more prudence, however you shall rue your actions while rotting in the pits." Stated one of the sprawled soldier's comrades.

Grignr's hand began to remove his blade from its

leather housing, but retarded the motion in face of the blades waving before his face.

"Dismiss your hand from the hilt, barbarbian, or you shall find a foot of steel sheathed in your gizzard."

Grignr weighed his position observing his plight, where-upon he took the soldier's advice as the only logical choice. To attempt to hack his way from his present predicament could only warrant certain death. He was of no mind to bring upon his own demise if an alternate path presented itself. The will to necessitate his life forced him to yield to the superior force in hopes of a moment of carlessness later upon the part of his captors in which he could effect a more plausible means of escape.

"You may steady your arms, I will go without a struggle."

"Your decision is a wise one, yet perhaps you would have been better off had you forced death," the soldier's mouth wrinkled to a sadistic grin of knowing mirth as he prodded his prisoner on with his sword point.

After an indiscriminate period of marching through slinking alleyways and dim moonlighted streets the procession confronted a massive seraglio. The palace area was surrounded by an iron grating, with a lush garden upon all sides.

The group was admitted through the gilded gateway and Grignr was ledalong a stone pathway bordered by plush vegitation lustfully enhanced by the moon's shimmering rays. Upon reaching the palace the group was granted entrance, and after several minutes of explanation, led through several winding corridors to a richly draped chamber.

Confronting the group was a short stocky man seated upon a golden throne. Tapestries of richly draped regal blue silk covered all walls of the chamber, while the steps leading to the throne were plated with sparkling white ivory. The man upon the throne had a naked wench seated at each of his arms, and a trusted advisor seated in back of him. At each cornwr of the chamber a guard stood at attention, with upraised pikes supported in their hands, golden chainmail adorning their torso's and barred helmets emitting scarlet plumes enshrouding their heads. The man rose from his throne to the dias surrounding it. His plush turquois robe dangled loosely from his chuncky frame.

The soldiers surrounding Grignr fell to their knees with heads bowed to the stone masonry of the floor in fearful dignity to their sovereign, leige.

"Explain the purpose of this intrusion upon my chateau!"

"Your sirenity, resplendent in noble grandeur, we have brought this yokel before you (the soldier gestured toward Grignr) for the redress or your all knowing wisdon in judgement regarding his fate."

"Down on your knees, lout, and pay proper homage to your sovereign!" commanded the pudgy noble of Grignr.

"By the surly beard of Mrifk, Grignr kneels to no man!" scowled the massive barbarian.

"You dare to deal this blasphemous act to me! You are

indeed brave stranger, yet your valor smacks of foolishness."

"I find you to be the only fool, sitting upon your pompous throne, enhancing the rolling flabs of your belly in the midst of your elaborate luxuryand ... " The soldier standing at Grignr's side smote him heavily in the face with the flat of his sword, cutting short the harsh words and knocking his battered helmet to the masonry with an echo-ing clang.

The paunchy noble's sagging round face flushed suddenly pale, then pastily lit up to a lustrous cherry red radiance. His lips trembled with malicious rage, while emitting a muffled sibilant gibberish. His sagging flabs rolled like a tub of upset jelly, then compressed as he sucked in his gut in an attempt to conceal his softness.

The prince regained his statue, then spoke to the soldiers surrounding Grignr, his face conforming to an ugly expression of sadistic humor.

"Take this uncouth heathen to the vault of misery, and be sure that his agonies are long and drawn out before death can release him."

"As you wish sire, your command shall be heeded immediately," answered the soldier on the right of Grignr as he stared into the barbarians seemingly unaffected face.

The advisor seated in the back of the noble slowly rose and advanced to the side of his master, motioning the wenches seated at his sides to remove themselves. He lowered his head and whispered to the noble.

"Eminence, the punishment you have decreed will cause much misery to this scum, yet it will last only a

short time, then release him to a land beyond the suffer-
ings of the human body. Why not mellow him in one of
the subterranean vaults for a few days, then send him to
life labor in one of your buried mines. To one such as he,
a life spent in the confinement of the stygian pits will be
an infinitely more appropiate and lasting torture."

The noble cupped his drooping double chin in the
folds of his briming palm, meditating for a moment
upon the rationality of the councilor's word's, then
raised his shaggy brown eyebrows and turned toward
the advisor, eyes aglow.

" . . . As always Agafnd, you speak with great wisdom.
Your words ring of great knowledge concerning the
nature of one such as he ," sayeth , the king. The noble
turned toward the prisoner with a noticable shimmer
reflecting in his frog-like eyes, and his lips contorting to
a greasy grin. "I have decided to void my previous
decree. The prisoner shall be removed to one of the
palaces underground vaults. There he shall stay until I
have decided that he has sufficiently simmered, where-
upon he is to be allowed to spend the remainder of his
days at labor in one of my mines."

Upon hearing this, Grignr realized that his fate would
be far less merciful than death to one such as he, who is
used to roaming the countryside at will. A life of confinement would be more than his body and mind could
stand up to. This type of life would be immeasurably
worse than death.

"I shall never understand the ways if your twisted
civilization. I simply defend my honor and am

condemned to life confinement, by a pig who sits on his royal ass wooing whores, and knows nothing of the affairs of the land he imagines to rule!" Lectures Grignr ?

"Enough of this! Away with the slut before I loose my control!"

Seeing the peril of his position, Grignr searched for an opening. Crushing prudence to the sward, he plowed into the soldier at his left arm taking hold of his sword, and bounding to the dias supporting the prince before the startled guards could regain their composure. Agafnd leaped Grignr and his sire, but found a sword blade permeating the length of his ribs before he could loosed his weapon.

The councilor slumped to his knees as Grignr slid his crimsoned blade from Agfnd's rib cage. The fat prince stood undulating in insurmountable fear before the edge of the fiery maned comet, his flabs of jellied blubber pulsating to and fro in ripples of flowing terror.

"Where is your wisdom and power now, your magjesty?" Growled Grignr.

The prince went rigid as Grignr discerned him glazing over his shoulder. He swlived to note the cause of the noble's attention, raised his sword over his head, and prepared to leash a vicious downward cleft, but fell short as the haft of a steel rimed pike clashed against his unguarded skull. Then blackness and solitude. Silence enshrouding and ever peaceful reind supreme.

"Before me, sirrah! Before me as always! Ha, Ha Ha, Haaaa . . . ", nobly cackled.

-3-

Consciousness returned to Grignr in stygmatic pools as his mind gradually cleared of the cobwebs cluttering its inner recesses, yet the stygian cloud of charcoal ebony remained. An incompatible shield of blackness, enhanced by the bleak abscense of sound.

Grignr's muddled brain reeled from the shock of the blow he had recieved to the base of his skull. The events leading to his predicament were slow to filter back to him. He dickered with the notion that he was dead and had descended or sunk, however it may be, to the shadowed land beyond the the aperature of the grave, but rejected this hypothesis when his memory sifted back within his grips. This was not the land of the dead, it was something infinitely more precarious than anything the grave could offer. Death promised an infinity of peace, not the finite misery of an inactive life of confined torture, forever concealed from the life bearing shafts of the beloved rising sun. The orb that had been before taken for granted, yet now cherished above all else. To be forever refused further glimpses of the snow capped summits of the land of his birth, never again to witness the thrill of plundering unexplored lands beyond the crest of a bleeding horizon, and perhaps worst of all the denial to ever again encompass the lustful excitement of caressing the naked curves of the body of a trim yound wench.

This was indeed one of the buried chasms of Hell concealed within the inner depths of the palace's despised interior. A fearful ebony chamber devised to drive to the brinks of insanity the minds of the unfortunately condemned, through the inapt solitude of a limbo of listless dreary silence.

-3 1/2-

A tightly rung elliptical circle or torches cast their wavering shafts prancing morbidly over the smooth surface of a rectangular, ridged alter. Expertly chiseled forms of grotesque gargoyles graced the oblique rim protruberating the length of the grim orifice of death, staring forever ahead into nothingness in complete ignorance of the bloody rites enacted in their prescence. Brown flaking stains decorated the golden surface of the ridge surrounding the alter, which banked to a small slit at the lower right hand corner of the altar. The slit stood above a crudely pounded pail which had several silver meshed chalices hanging at its sides. Dangling at the rimof golden mallet, the handle of which was engraved with images of twisted faces and groved at its far end with slots designed for a snug hand grip. The head of the mallet was slightly larger than a clenched fist and shaped into a smooth oval mass.

Encircling the marble altar was a congregation of leering shamen. Eerie chants of a bygone age, originating unknown eons before the memory of man, were being uttered from the buried recesses of the acolytes' deep lings. Orange paint was smeared in generous globules over the tops of thw Priests' wrinkled shaven scalps, while golden rings projected from the lobes of their pink ears. Ornate robes of lusciour purple satin enclosed their bulging torsos, attached around their waists with silvered silk lashes latched with ebony buckles in the shape of morose mis-shaped skulls. Dangling around their necks were oval fashoned medalions held by thin gold chains, featuring in their centers blood red rubys which resembled crimson fetish eyeballs. Cushoning their bare feet were plush red felt slippers with pointed golden spikes projecting from their tips.

Situated in front of the altar, and directly adjacent to the copper pail was a massive jade idol; a misshaped, hideous bust of the shamens' pagan diety. The shimmering green idol was placed in a sitting posture on an ornately carved golden throne raised upon a round, dvory plated dias; it bulging arms and webbed hands resting on the padded arms of the seat. Its head was entwined in golden snake-like coils hanging over its oblong ears, which tappered off to thin hollow points. Its nose was a bulging triangular mass, sunken in at its sides with tow gaping nostrils. Dramatic beneath the nostrils was a twisted, shaggy lipped mouth, giving the impression of a slovering sadistic grimace.

At the foot of the heathen diety a slender, pale faced female, naked but for a golden, jeweled harness enshrouding her huge outcropping breasts, supporting long silver laces which extended to her thigh, stood before the pearl white field with noticable shivers traveling up and down the length of her exquisitely molded body. Her delicate lips trembled beneath soft narrow hands as she attemped to conceal herself from the piercing stare of the ambivalent idol.

Glaring directly down towards her was the stoney, cycloptic face of the bloated diety. Gaping from its single obling socket was scintillating, many fauceted scarlet emerald, a brilliant gem seeming to possess a life all of its own. A priceless gleaming stone, capable of domineering the wealth of conquering empires . . . the eye of Argon.

-4-

All knowledge of measuring time had escaped Grignr. When a person is deprived of the sun, moon, and stars, he looses all conception of time as he had previously understood it. It seemed as if years had passed if time were being measured by terms of misery and mental anguish, yet he estimated that his stay had only been a few days in length. He has slept three times and had been fed five times since his awakening in the crypt. However, when the actions of the body are restricted its needs are also affected. The need for nourishmnet and slumber are directly proportional to the functions the body has performed, meaning that when free and active Grignr may become hungry every six hours and witness the desire for sleep every fifteen hours, whereas in his present condition he may encounter the need for food every ten hours, and the want for rest every twenty hours. All methods he had before depended upon were extinct in the dismal pit. Hence, he may have been imprisoned for ten minutes or ten years, he did not know, resulting in a disheartened emotion deep within his being.

The food, if you can honor the moldering lumps of fetid mush to that extent, was born to him by two guards who opened a portal at the top of his enclosure and shoved it to him in wooden bowls, retrieving the food and water bowels from his previous meal at the same time, after which they threw back the bolts on the iron latch and returned to their other duties. Since deprived of all other means of nourishment, Grignr was impelled to eat the tainted slop in order to ward off the paings of starvation, though as he stuffed it into his mouth with his filthy fingers and struggled to force it down his throat, he imagined it was that which had been spurned by the hounds stationed at various segments of the palace.

There was little in the baren vault that could occupy his body or mind. He had paced out the length and width of the enclosure time and time again and tested every granite slab which consisted the walls of the prison in hopes of finding a hidden passage to freedom, all of which was to no avail other than to keep him busy and distract his mind from wandering to thoughts of what he believed was his future. He had memorized the number of strides from one end to the other of the cell, and knew the exact number of slabs which made up the bleak dungeon. Numorous schemes were introduced and alternately discarded in turn as they succored to unravel to him no means of escape which stood the slightest chance of sucess.

Anguish continued to mount as his means of occupation were rapidly exhausted. Suddenly without no tive, he wasrouted from his contemplations as he detected a faint scratching sound at the end of the crypt opposite him. The sound seemed to be caused by something trying to scrape away at the grantite blocks the floor of the enclosure consisted of, the sandy scratching of something like an animal's claws.

Grignr gradually groped his way to the other end of the vault carefully feeling his way along with his hands ahead of him. When a few inches from the wall, a loud, penetrating squeal, and the scampering of small padded feet reverberated from the walls of the roughly hewn chamber.

Grignr threw his hands up to shield his face, and flung himself backwards upon his buttocks. A fuzzy form bounded to his hairy chest, burying its talons in his flesh while gnashing toward his throat with its grinding white teeth;its sour, fetid breath scortching the sqirming barbarians dilating nostrils. Grignr grappled with the lashing flexor muscles of the repugnant body of a garganuan brownhided rat, striving to hold its razor teeth from his juicy jugular, as its beady grey organs of sight glazed into the flaring emeralds of its prey.

Taking hold of the rodent around its lean, growling stomach with both hands Grignr pried it from his crimson rent breast, removing small patches of flayed flesh from his chest in the motion between the squalid black claws of the starving beast. Holding the rodent at arms length, he cupped his righthand over its frothing face, contrcting his fingers into a vice-like fist over the quivering head. Retaining his grips on the rat, grignr flexed his outstretched arms while slowly twisting his right hand clockwise and his left hand counter clockwise motion. The rodent let out a tortured squall, drawing scarlet as it violently dug its foam flecked fangs into the barbarians sweating palm, causing his face to contort to an ugly grimace as he cursed beneath his braeth.

With a loud crack the rodents head parted from its squirming torso, sending out a sprinking shower of crimson gore, and trailing a slimy string of disjointed vertebrae, snapped trachea, esophagus, and jugular, disjointed hyoid bone, morose purpled stretched hide, and blood seared muscles.

Flinging the broken body to the floor, Grignr shook his blood streaked hands and wiped them against his thigh until dry, then wiped the blood that had showered his face and from his eyes. Again sitting himself upon the jagged floor, he prepared to once more revamp his glum meditations. He told himself that as long as he still breathed the gust of life through his lungs, hope was not lost; he told himself this, but found it hard to comprehend in his gloomy surroundings. Yet he was still alive, his bulging sinews at their peak of marvel, his struggling mind floating in a miral of impressed excellence of thought. Plot after plot sifted through his mind in energetic contemplations.

Then it hit him. Minutes may have passed in silent thought or days, he could not tell, but he stumbled at last upon a plan that he considered as holding a slight margin of plausibility.

He might die in the attempt, but he knew he would not submit without a final bloody struggle. It was not a foolproof plan, yet it built up a store of renewed vortexed energy in his overwroughtsoul, though he might perish in the execution of the escape, he would still be escaping the life of infinite torture in store forhim. Either way he would still cheat the gloating prince of the succored revenge his sadistic mind craved so dearly.

The guards would soon come to bear him off to the prince's buried mines of dread, giving him the sought after opportunity to execute his newly formulated plan. Groping his way along the rough floor Grignr finally found his tool in a pool of congealed gore; the carcass of the decapitated rodent; the tool that the very filth he had been sentenced too, spawned. When the time came for action he would have to be prepared, so he set himself to rending the sticky hulk in grim silence, searching by the touch of his fingertips for the lever to freedom.

-5-

"Up to the altar and be done with it wench;" ordered a fidgeting shaman as he gave the female a grim stare accompanied by the wrinkling of his lips to a mirthful grin of delight.

The girl burst into a slow steady whimper, stooping shakily to her knees and cringing woefully from the priest with both arms wound snake-like around the bulging jade jade shin rising before her scantily attired figure. Her face was redly inflamed from the salty flow of tears spouting from her glassy dilated eyeballs.

With short, heavy footfals the priest approached the female, his piercing stare never wavering from her quivering young countenance. Halting before the terrified girl he projected his arm outward and motioned her to arise with an upward movement of his hand. the girl's whimpering increased slightly and she sunk closer to the floor rather than arising. The flickering torches outlined her trim build with a weird ornate glow as it cast a ghostly shadow dancing in horrid waves of splendor over smoothly worn whiteness of the marble hewn altar.

The shaman's lips curled back farther, exposing a set of blackened, decaying molars which transformed his slovenly grin into a wide greasy arc of sadistic mirth and alternately interposed into the female a strong sensation of stomach curdling nausea. "Have it as you will female;" gloated the enhanced priest as he bent over at the waist, projecting his ape-like arms forward, and clasped the female's slender arms with his hairy round fists. With an inward surge of of his biceps he harshly jerked the trembling girl to her feet and smothered her salty wet cheeks with the moldy touch of his decrepid, dull red lips.

The vile stench of the Shaman's hot fetid breath over came the nauseated female with a deep soul searing sickness, causing her to wrench her head backwards and regurgitate a slimy, orangewhite stream of swelling gore over the richly woven purple robe of the enthused acolyte.

The priest's lips trembled with a malicious rage as he removed his callous paws from the girl's arms and replaced them with tightly around her undulating neck, shaking her violently to and fro.

The girl gasped a tortured groan from her clamped lungs, her sea blue eyes bulging forth from damp sockets. Cocking her right foot backwards, she leashed it desperately outwards with the strength of a demon possessed, lodging her sandled foot squarely between the shaman's testicles.

The startled priest released his crushing grip, crimping his body over at the waist overlooking his recessed belly; wide open in a deep chasim. His face flushed to a rose red shade of crimson, eyelids fluttering wide with eyeballs protruding blindly outwards from their sockets to their outmost perimeters, while his lips quivered wildly about allowing an agonized wallow to gust forth as his breath billowed from burning lungs. His hands reached out clutching his urinary gland as his knees wobbled rapidly about for a few seconds then buckled, causing the ruptured shaman to collapse in an egg huddled mass to the granite pavement, rolling helplessly about in his agony.

The pathetic screeches of the shaman groveling in dejected misery upon the hand hewn granite laid pavement, worn smooth by countless hours of arduous sweat and toil, a welter of ichor oozing through his clenched hands, attracted the purturbed attention of his comrades from their foetid ulations. The actions of this this rebellious wench bespoke the creedence of an unheard of sacrilige. Never before in a lost maze of untold eons had a chosen one dared to demonstrate such blasphemy in the face of the cult's idolic diety.

The girl cowered in unreasoning terror, helpless in the face of the emblazoned acolytes' rage; her orchid tusseled face smothered betwixt her bulging bosom as she shut her curled lashed tightly hoping to open them and find herself awakening from a morbid nightmare. yet the hand of destiny decreed her no such mercy, the antagonized pack of leering shaman converging tensely upon her prostrate form were entangled all too lividly in the grim web of reality.

Shuddering from the clamy touch of the shaman as they grappled with her supple form, hands wrenching at her slender arms and legs in all directions, her bare body being molested in the midst of a labyrnth of orange smudges, purpled satin, and mangled skulls, shadowed in an eerie crimson glow; her confused head reeled then clouded in a mist of enshrouding ebony as she lapsed beneath the protective sheet of unconsiousness to a land peach and resign.

-6-

"Take hold of this rope," said the first soldier, "and climb out from your pit, slut. Your presence is requested in another far deeper hell hole."

Grignr slipped his right hand to his thigh, concealing a small opaque object beneath the folds of the g-string wrapped about his waist. Brine wells swelled in Grignr's cold, jade squinting eyes, which grown accustomed to the gloom of the stygian pools of ebony engulfing him, were bedazzled and blinded by flickerering radiance cast forth by the second soldiers's resin torch.

Tightly gripped in the second soldier's right hand, opposite the intermittent torch, was a large double edged axe, a long leather wound oaken handled transfixing the center of the weapon's iron head. Adorning the torso's of both of the sentries were thin yet sturdy hauberks, the breatplates of which were woven of tightly hemmed twines of reinforced silver braiding. Cupping the soldiers' feet were thick leather sandals, wound about their shins to two inches below their knees. Wrapped about their waists were wide satin girdles, with slender bladed poniards dangling loosely from them, the hilts of which featured scarlet encrusted gems. Resting upon the manes of their heads, and reaching midway to their brows were smooth copper morions. Spiraling the lower portion of the helmet were short, up-curved silver spikes, while a golden hump spired from the top of each basinet. Beneath their chins, wound around their necks, and draping their clad shoulders dangled regal purple satin cloaks, which flowed midway to the soldiers feet.

hand over hand, feet braced against the dank walls of the enclosure, huge Grignr ascended from the moldering dephs of the forlorn abyss. His swelled limbs, stiff due to the boredom of a timeless inactivity, compounded by the musty atmosture and jagged granite protuberan against his body, craved for action. The opportunity now presenting itself served the purpose of oiling his rusty joints, and honing his dulled senses.

He braced himself, facing the second soldier. The sentry's stature was was wildly exaggerated in the glare of the flickering cresset cuppex in his right fist. His eyes were wide open in a slightly slanted owlish glaze, enhanced in their sinister intensity by the hawk-bill curve of his nose andpale yellow pique of his cheeks.

"Place your hands behind your back," said the second soldier as he raised his ax over his right shoulder blade and cast it a wavering glance. "We must bind your wrists to parry any attempts at escape. Be sure to make the knot a stout one, Broig, we wouldn't want our guest to take leave of our guidance."

Broig grasped Grignr's left wrist and reached for the barbarians's right wrist. Grignr wrenched his right arm free and swiveled to face Broig, reach- beneath his loin cloth with his right hand. The sentry grappled at his girdle for the sheathed dagger, but recoiled short of his intentions as Grignr's right arm swept to his gorge. The soldier went limp, his bobbing eyes rolling beneath fluttering eyelids, a deep welt across his spouting gullet. Without lingering to observe the result of his efforts, Grignr dropped to his knees. The second soldier's axe cleft over Grignr's head in a blze of silvered ferocity, severing several scarlet locks from his scalp. Coming to rest in his fellow's stomach, the iron head crashed through mail and flesh with splintering force, spilling a pool of crimsoned entrails over the granite paving.

Before the sentry could wrench his axe free from his comrade's carcass, he found Grignr's massive hands clasped about his throat, choking the life from his clamped lungs. With a zealous grunt, the Ecordian flexed his tightly corded biceps, forcing the grim faced soldier to one knee. The sentry plunged his right fist into Grignr's face, digging his grimy nails into the barbarians flesh. Ejaculating a curse through rasping teeth, grignr surged the bulk of his weight foreard, bowling the beseiged soldier over upon his back. The sentry's arms collapsed to his thigh, shuddering convulsively; his bulging eyes staring blindly from a bloated ,cherry red face.

Rising to his feet, Grignr shook the bllod from his eyes, ruffling his surly red mane as a brush fire swaying to the nightime breeze. Stooping over the spr sprawled corpse of the first soldier, Grignr retrieved a small white object from a pool of congealing gore. Snorting a gusty billow of mirth, he once more concealed th e tiny object beneath his loin cloth; the tediously honed pelvis bone of the broken rodent. Returning his attention toward the second soldier, Grignr turned to the task of attiring his limbs. To move about freely through the dim recesses of the castle would require the grotesque garb of its soldiery.

Utilizing the silence and stealth aquired in the untamed climbs of his childhood, Grignr slink through twisting corridors, and winding stairways, lighting his way with the confisticated torch of his dispatched guardian. Knowing where his steps were leading to, Grignr meandered aimlessly in search of an exit from the chateau's dim confines. The wild blood coarsing through his veins yearned for the undefiled freedom of the livid wilderness lands.

Coming upon a fork in the passage he treaked, voices accompanied by clinking footfalls discerned to his sensitive ears from the left corridor. Wishing to avoid contact, Grignr veered to the right passageway. If aquested as to the purpose of his presence, his barbarous accent would reveal his identity, being that his attire was not that of the castle's mercenary troops.

In grim silence Grignr treaded down the dingily lit corridor; a stalking panther creeping warily along on padded feet. After an interminable period of wandering through the dull corridors; no gaps to break the monotony of the cold gray walls, Grignr espied a small winding stairway. Descending the flight of arced granite slabs to their posterior, Grignr was confronted by a short haalway leading to a tall arched wooden doorway.

Halting before the teeming portal portal, Grignr restes his shaggy head sideways against the barrier. Detecting no sounds from within, he grasped the looped metel handle of the door; his arms surging with a tremendous effort of bulging muscles, yet the door would not budge. Retrieving his ax from where he had sheathed it beneath his girdle, he hefted it in his mighty hands with an apiesed grunt, and wedging one of its blackened edges into the crack between the portal and its iron rimed sill. Bracing his sandaled right foot against the rougjly hewn wall, teeth tightly clenched, Grignr appilevered the oaken haft, employing it as a lever whereby to pry open the barrier. The leather wound hilt bending to its utmost limits of endurance, the massive portal swung open with a grating of snapped latch and rusty iron hinges.

Glancing about the dust swirled room in the gloomily dancing glare of his flickering cresset, Grignr eyed evidences of the enclosure being nothing more than a forgotten storeroom. Miscellaneous articles required for the maintainance of a castle were piled in disorganized heaps at infrequent intervals toward the wall opposite the barbarian's piercing stare. Utilizing long, bounding strides, Grignr paced his way over to the mounds of supplies to discover if any articles of value were contained within their midst.

Detecting a faint clinking sound, Grignr sprawed to his left side with the speed of a striking cobra, landing harshly upon his back; torch and axe loudly clattering to the floor in a morass of sparks and flame. A elmwoven board leaped from collapsed flooring, clashing against the jagged flooring and spewing a shower of orange and yellow sparks over Grignr's startled face. Rising uneasily to his feet, the half stunned Ecordian glared down at the grusome arm of death he had unwittingly sprung. "Mrifk!"

If not for his keen auditory organs and lighting steeled reflexes, Grignr would have been groping through the shadowed hell-pits of the Grim Reaper. He had unknowingly stumbled upon an ancient, long forgotton booby trap; a mistake which would have stunted the perusal of longevity of one less agile. A mechanism, similar in type to that of a minature catapult was concealed beneath two collapsable sections of granite flooring. The arm of the device was four feet long, boasting razor like cleats at regular intervals along its face with which it was to skewer the luckless body of its would be victim. Grignr had stepped upon a concealed catch which relaesed a small metal latch beneath the two granite sections, causing them to fall inward, and thereby loose the spiked arm of death they precariously held in.

Partially out of curiosity and partially out of an inordinate fear of becoming a pincushion for a possible second trap, Grignr plunged his torch into the exposed gap in the floor. The floor of a second chamber stood out seven feet below the glare. Tossing his torch through the aperature, Grignr grasped the side of an adjoining tile, dropping down.

Glancing about the room, Grignr discovered that he had decended into the palace's mausoleum. Rectangular stone crypts cluttered the floor at evenly placed intervals. The tops of the enclosures were plated with thick layers of virgin gold, while the sides were plated with white ivory; at one time sparkling, but now grown dingy through the passage of the rays of allencompassing mother time. Featured at the head of each sarcophagus in tarnished silver was an expugnisively carved likeness of its rotting inhabitant.

A dingy atmosphere pervaded the air of the chamber; which sealed in the enclosure for an unknown period had grown thick and stale. Intermingling with the curdled currents was the repugnant stench of slowly moldering flesh, creeping ever slowly but surely through minute cracks in the numerous vaults. Due to the embalming of the bodies, their flesh decayed at a much slower rate than is normal, yet the nauseous oder was none the less repellant.

Towering over Grignr's head was the trap he released. The mechanism of the miniaturized catapolt was cluttered with mildew and cobwebs. Notwithstanding these relics of antiquity, its efficiency remained unimpinged. To the right of the trap wound a short stairway through a recess in the ceiling; a concealed entrance leading to the mausoleum for which the catapult had obviously been erected as a silent, relentless guardian.

Climbing up the side of the device, Grignr set to the task of resetting its mechanism. In the e event that a search was organized, it would prove well to leave no evidence of his presence open to wandering eyes. Besides, it might even serve to dwindle the size of an opposing force.

Descending from his perch, Grignr was startled by a faintly muffled scream of horrified desperation. His hair prickled yawkishly in disorganized clumps along his scalp. As a cold danced along the length of his spinal cord. No moral/mortal barrier, human or otherwise, was capable of arousing the numbing sensation of fear inside of Grignr's smoldering soul. However, he was overwrought by the forces of the barbarians' instinctive fear of the supernatural. His mighty thews had always served to adequately conquer any tangible foe., but the intangible was something distant and terrible. Dim horrifying tales passed by word of mouth over glimmering camp fires and skins of wine had more than once served the purpose of chilling the marrowed core of his sturdy limbed bones.

Yet, the scream contained a strangely human quality, unlike that which Grignr imagined would come from the lungs of a demon or spirit, making Grignr take short nervous strides advancing to the sarcophagus from which the sound was issuing. Clenching his teeth in an attempt to steel his jangled nerves, Grignr slid the engraved slab from the vault with a sharp rasp of grinding stone. Another long drawn cry of terror infested anguish met the barbarian, scoring like the shrill piping of a demented banshee; piercing the inner fibres of his superstitious brain with primitive dread dread and awe.

Stooping over to espy the tomb's contents, the glittering Ecordians nostrills were singed by the scorching aroma of a moldering corpse, long shut up and fermenting; the same putrid scent which permeated the entire chamber, though multiplied to a much more concentrated dosage. The shriveled, leathery packet of crumbling bones and dried flacking flesh offered no resistance, but remained in a fixed position of perpetual vigilance, watching over its dim abode from hollow gaping sockets.

The tortured crys were not coming from the tomb but from some hidden depth below! Pulling the reaking corpse from its resting place, Grignr tossed it to the floor in a broken, mangled heap. Upon one side of the crypt's bottom was attached a series of tiny hinges while running parallel along the opposite side of a convex railing like protruberance; laid so as to appear as a part of the interior surface of the sarcophagus.

Raising the slab upon its bronze hinges, long removed from the gaze of human eyes, Grignr percieved a scene which caused his blood to smolder not unlike bubbling, molten lava. Directly below him a whimpering female lay stretched upon a smooth surfaced marble altar. A pack of grasy faced shamen clustered around her in a tight circular formation. Crouched over the girl was a tall, potbellied priest; his face dominated by a disgusting, open mouthed grimace of sadistic glee. Suspended from the acolyte's clenched right hand was a carven oval faced mallet, which he waved menacingly over the girl's shadowed face; an incoherent gibberish flowing from his grinning, thick lipped mouth.

In the face of the amorphos, broad breated female, stretched out aluringly before his gaping eyes; the universal whim of nature filing a plea of despair inside of his white hot soul; Grignr acted in the only manner he could perceive. Giving vent to a hoarse, throat rending battle cry, Grignr plunged into the midst of the startled shamen; torch simmering in his left hand andax twirling in his right hand.

A gaunt skull faced priest standing at the far side of the altar clutched desperately at his throat, coughing furiously in an attempt to catch his breath. Lurching helplessly to and fro, the acolyte pitched headlong against the gleaming base of a massive jade idol. Writhing agonizedly against the hideous image, foam flecking his chalk white lips, the priest struggled help-lessly — the victim of an epileptic siezure.

Startled by the barbarians stunning appearance, the chronic fit of their fellow, and the fear that Grignr might be the avantgarde of a conquering force dedicated to the cause of destroying their degenerated cult, the saman momentarily lost their composure. Giving vent to heed-less pandemonium, the priests fell easy prey to Grignr's sweeping arc of crimsoned death and maiming distruction.

The acolyte performing the sacrifice took a vicious blow to the stomach; hands clutching vitals and severed spinal cord as he sprawled over the altar. The disor anized priests lurched and staggered with split skulls, dismembered limbs, and spewing entrails before the enraged Ecordian's relentless onslaught. The howles of the maimed and dying reverberated against the walls of the tiny chamber; a chorus of hell frought despair; as the granite floor ran red with blood. The entire chamber was encompassed in the heat of raw savage butchery as Grignr luxuriated in the grips of a primitive, beastly blood lust.

Presently all went silenet save for the ebbing groans of the sinking shaman and Grignr's heaving breath accompanied by several gusty curses. The well had run dry. No more lambs remained for the slaughter.

The rampaging stead of death having taken of Grignr for the moment, left the barbarian free to the exploitation of his other perusials. Towering over his head was the misshaped image of the cult's hideous diety — Argon. The fantastic size of the idol in consideration of its being of pure jade was enough to cause the senses of any man to stagger and reel, yet thus was not the case for the behemoth. he had paid only casual notice to this incredible fact, while riviting the whole of his attention upon the jewel protruding from the idol's sole socket; its masterfully cut faucets emitting blinding rays of hypnotising beauty. After all, a man cannot slink from a heavily guarded palace while burdened down by the intense bulk of a squatting statue, providing of course that the

THE EYE OF ARGON

idol can even be hefted, which in fact was beyond the reaches of Grignr's coarsing stamina. On the other hand, the jewel, gigantic as it was, would not present a hinderence of any mean concern.

"Help me ... please ... I can make it well worth your while," pleaded a soft, anguish strewn voice wafting over Grignr's shoulders as he plucked the dull red emerald from its roots. Turning, Grignr faced the female that had lured him into this blood bath, but whom had become all but forgotten in the heat of the battle.

"You"; ejaculated the Ecordian in a pleased tone. "I though that I had seen the last of you at the tavern, but verilly I was mistaken." Grignr advanced into the grips of the female's entrancing stare, severing the golden chains that held her captive upon the altars highly polished face of ornamental limestone.

As Grignr lifted the girl from the altar, her arms wound dexterously about his neck; soft and smooth against his harsh exterior. "Art thou pleased that we have chanced to meet once again?" Grignr merely voiced an sighed grunt, returning the damsels embrace while he smothered her trim, delicate lips between the coarsing protrusions of his reeking maw.

"Let us take leave of this retched chamber." Stated Grignr as he placed the female upon her feet. She swooned a moment, causing Grignr to giver her support then regained her stance. "Art thou able to find your way through the accursed passages of this castle? Mrifk! Every one of the corridors of this damned place are identical."

"Aye; I was at one time a slave of prince Agaphim. His clammy touch sent a sour swill through my belly, but my efforts reaped a harvest. I gained the pig's liking whereby he allowed me the freedom of the palace. It was through this means that I eventually managed escape at the western gate. His trust found him with a dagger thrust his ribs," the wench stated whimsicoracally.

"What were you doing at the tavern whence I discovered you?" asked Grignr as he lifted the female through the opening into the mausoleum.

"I had sought to lay low from the palace's guards as they conducted their search for me. The tavern was seldom frequented by the palace guards and my identity was unknown to the common soldiers. It was through the disturbance that you caused that the palace guards were attracted to the tavern. I was dragged away shortly after you were escorted to the palace."

"What are you called by female?"

"Carthena, daughter of Minkardos, Duke of Barwego, whose lands border along the northwestern fringes of Gorzom. I was paid as homage to Agaphim upon his thirty-eighth year," husked the femme!

"And I am called a barbarian!" Grunted Grignr in a disgusted tone!

"Aye! The ways of our civilization are in many ways warped and distorted, but what is your calling," she queried, bustily?

"Grignr of Ecordia."

"Ah, I have heard vaguely of Ecordia. It is the hill country to the far east of the Noregolean Empire. I have also heard Agaphim curse your land more than once when his troops were routed in the unaccustomed mountains and gorges." Sayeth she.

"Aye. My people are not tarnished by petty luxuries and baubles. They remain fierce and unconquerable in their native climes." After reaching the hidden panel at the head of the stairway, Grignr was at a loss in regard to its operation. His fiercest heaves were as pebbles against burnished armour! Carthena depressed a small symbol included within the elaborate design upon the panel whereopen it slowly slid into a cleft in the wall. "How did you come to be the victim of those crazed shamen?" Quested Grignr as he escorted Carthena through the piles of rummage on the left side of the trap.

"By Agaphim's orders I was thrust into a secluded cell to await his passing of sentence. By some means, the Priests of Argon acquired a set of keys to the cell. They slew the guard placed over me and abducted me to the chamber in which you chanced to come upon the scozsctic sacrifice. Their hell-spawned cult demands a sacrifice once every three moons upon its full journey through the heavens. They were startled by your unannounced appearance through the fear that you had been sent by Agaphim. The prince would surely have submitted them to the most ghastly of tortures if he had ever discovered their unfaithfulness to Sargon, his bastard diety. Many of the partakers of the ritual were high nobles and high trustees of the inner palace; Agaphim's pittiless wrath would have been unparalled."

"They have no more to fear of Agaphim now!" Bellowed Grignr in a deep mirthful tome; a gleeful smirk upon his face. "I have seen that they were delivered from his vengence."

Engrossed by Carthena's graceful stride and conversation Grignr failed to take note of the footfalls rapidly approaching behind him. As he swung aside the arched portal linking the chamber with the corridors beyond, a maddened, blood lusting screech reverberated from his ear drums. Seemingly utilizing the speed of thought, Grignr swiveled to face his unknown foe. With gaping eyes and widened jaws, Grignr raised his axe above his surly mein; but he was too late.

-7-

With wobbling knees and swimming head, the priest that had lapsed into an epileptic siezure rose unsteadily to his feet. While enacting his choking fit in writhing agony, the shaman was overlooked by Grignr. The barbarian had mistaken the siezure for the death throes of the acolyte, allowing the priest to avoid his stinging blade. The sight that met the priests inflamed eyes nearly served to sprawl him upon the floor once more. The sacrificial sat it grim, blood splattered silence all around him, broken only by the occasional yelps and howles of his maimed and butchered fellows. Above his head rose the hideous idol, its empty socket holding the shaman's ifurbished infuriated gaze.

His eyes turned to a stoney glaze with the realization of the pillage and blasphemy. Due to his high succeptibility following the siezure, the priest was transformed into a raving maniac bent soley upon reaking vengeance. With lips curled and quivering, a crust of foam dripping from them, the acolyte drew a long, wicked looking jewel hilted scimitar from his silver girdle and fled through the aperature in the ceiling uttering a faintly perceptible ceremonial jibberish.

-7 1/2-

A sweeping scimitar swung towards Grignr's head in a shadowed blur of motion. With Axe raised over his head, Grignr prepared to parry the blow, while gaping wideeyed in open mouthed perplexity. Suddenly a sharp snap resounded behind the frothing shaman. The scimitar, halfway through its fatal sweep, dropped from a quivering nerveless hand, clattering harmlessly to the stoneage. Cutting his screech short with a bubbling, red mouthed gurgle, the lacerated acolyte staggered under the pressure of the released spring-board. After a moment of hopeless struggling, the shaman buckled, sprawling face down in a widening pool of bllod and entrails, his regal purple robe blending enhancingly with the swirling streams of crimson.

"Mrifk! I thought I had killed the last of those dogs;" muttered Grignr in a half apathetic state.

"Nay Grignr. You doubtless grew careless while giving vent to your lusts. But let us not tarry any long lest we over tax the fates. The paths leading to freedom will soon be barred.

The wretch's crys must certainly have attracted unwanted attention," the wench mused.

"By what direction shall we pursue our flight?"

"Up that stair and down the corridor a short distance is the concealed enterance to a tunnel seldom used by others than the prince, and known to few others save the palace's royalty. It is used mainly by the prince when he wishes to take leave of the palace in secret. It is not always in the Prince's best interests to leave his chateau in public view. Even while under heavy guard he is often assaulted by hurtling stones and rotting fruits. The commoners have little love for him." lectured the nerelady!

"It is amazing that they would ever have left a pig like him become their ruler. I should imagine that his people would rise up and crucify him like the dog he is."

"Alas, Grignr, it is not as simple as all that. His soldiers are well paid by him. So long as he keeps their wages up they will carry out his damned wished. The crude impliments of the commonfolk would never stand up under an onslaught of forged blades and protective armor; they would be going to their own slaughter," stated Carthena to a confused, but angered Grignr as they topped the stairway.

"Yet how can they bear to live under such oppression? I would sooner die beneath the sword than live under such a dog's command." added Grignr as the pair stalked down the hall in the direction opposite that in which Grignr had come.

"But all men are not of the same mold that you are born of, they choose to live as they are so as to save their filthy necks from the chopping block." Returned Carthena in a disgusted tone as she cast an appiesed glance towards the stalwart figure at her side whose left arm was wound dextrously about her slim waist; his slowly waning torch casting their images in intermingling wisps as it dangled from his left hand.

Presently Carthena came upon the panel, concealed amonst the other granite slabs and discernable only by the burned out cresset above it. "As I push the cresset aside push the panel inwards." Catrhena motioned to the panel she was refering to and twisted the cresset in a counterclockwise motion. Grignr braced his right shoulder against the walling, concentrating the force of his bulk against it. The slab gradually swung inward with a slight grating sound. Carthena stooped beneath Grignr's corded arms and crawled upon all fours into the passage beyond. Grignr followed after easing the slab back into place.

Winding before the pair was a dark musty tunnel, exhibiting tangled spider webs from it ceiling to wall and an oozing, sickly slime running lazily upon its floor. Hanging from the chipped wall upon GrignR's right side was a half mouldered corpse, its grey flacking arms held in place by rusted iron manacles. Carthena flinched back into Grignr's arms at sight of the leering set in an ugly distorted grimmace; staring horribly at her from hollow gaping sockets.

"This alcove must also be used by Agaphim as a

torture chamber. I wonder how many of his enemies have disappeared into these haunts never to be heard from again," pondered the hulking brute.

"Let us flee before we are also caught within Agaphim's ghastly clutches. The exit from this tunnel cannot be very far from here!" Said Carthena with a slight sob to her voice, as she sagged in Grignr's encompasing embrace.

"Aye; It will be best to be finished with this corridor as soon as it is possible. But why do you flinch from the sight of death so? Mrift! You have seen much death this day without exhibiting such emotions." Exclaimed Grignr as he led her trembling form along the dingy confines.

"—The man hanging from the wall was Doyanta. He had committed the folly of showing affections for me in front of Agaphim — he never meant any harm by his actions!" At this Carthena broke into a slow steady whimpering, chokking her voice with gasping sobs. "There was never anything between us yet Agaphim did this to him! The beast! May the demons of Hell's deepest haunts claw away at his wretched flesh for this merciless act!" she prayed.

"I detect that you felt more for this fellow than you wish to let on ... but enough of this, We can talk of such matters after we are once more free to do so." With this Grignr lifted the grieved female to her feet and strode onward down the corridor, supporting the bulk of her weight with his surging left arm.

Presently a dim light was perceptibly filtering into the tunnel, casting a dim reddish hue upon the moldy wall of the passage's grim confines. Carthena had ceased her whimpering and partially regained her composure. "The tunnel's end must be nearing. Rays of sunlight are beginning to seep into . . . "

Grignr clameed his right hand over Carthena's mouth and with a slight struggle pulled her over to the shadows at the right hand wall of the path, while at the same time thrusting this torch beneath an overhanging stone to smother its flickering rays. "Be silent; I can hear footfalls approaching through the tunnel;" growled Grignr in a hushed tone.

"All that you hear are the horses corraled at the far end of the tunnel. That is a further sign that we are nearing our goal." She stated!

"All that you hear is less than I hear! I heard footsteps coming towards us. Silence yourself that we may find out whom we are being brought into contact with. I doubt that any would have thought as yet of searching this passage for us. The advantage of surprize will be upon our side." Grignr warned.

Carthena cast her eyes downward and ceased any further pursuit towards conversation, an irritating habit in which she had gained an amazing proficiency. Two figures came into the pairs view, from around a turn in the tunnel. They were clothed in rich luxuriant silks and rambling o on in conversation while ignorant of their crouching foes waiting in an ambush ahead.

" . . . That barbarian dog is cringing beneath the weight of the lash at this moment sire. He shall cause no more disturbance."

"Aye, and so it is with any who dare to cross the path of Sargon's chosen one." said the 2nd man.

"But the peasants are showing signs of growing unrest. They complain that they cannot feet their families while burdened with your taxes."

"I shall teach those sluts the meaning of humility! Order an immediate increase upon their taxes. They dare to question my sovereign authority, Ha-a, they shall soon learn what true oppression can be. I will . . . "

A shodowed bulk leapt from behind a jutting promontory as it brought down a double edged axe with the spped of a striking thought. One of the nobles sagged lifeless to the ground, skull split to the teeth.

Grignr gasped as he observed the bisected face set in its leering death agonies. It was Agafnd! The dead mans comrade having recovered from his shock drew a jewel encrusted dagger from beneath the folds of his robe and lunged toward the barbarians back. Grignr spun at the sound from behind and smashed down his crimsoned axe once more. His antagonist lunged howling to a stream of stagnent green water, grasping a spouting stump that had once been a wrist. Grignr raised his axe over his head and prepared to finish the incomplete job, but was detered half way through his lunge by a frenzied screech from behind.

Carthena leapt to the head of the writhing figure, plunging a smoldering torch into the agonized face. The howls increased in their horrid intensity, stifled by the sizzling of roasting flesh, then died down until the man was reduced to a blubbering mass of squirming, insensate flesh.

Grignr advance to Carthena's side wincing slightly from the putrid aroma of charred flesh that rose in a puff of thick white smog throughout the chamber. Carthena reeled slightly, staring dasedly downward at her gruesome handywork. "I had to do it … it was Agaphim … I had to," she exclaimed!

"Sargon should be more carful of his right hand men." Added Grignr, a smug grin upon his lips. "But to hell with Sargon for now, the stench is becoming bothersome to me." With that Grignr grasped Carthena around the waist leading her around the bend in the cave and into the open.

A ball of feral red was rising through the mists of the eastern horizon, disipating the slinking shadows of the night. A coral stood before the pair, enclosing two grazing mares. Grignr reached into a weighted down leather pouch dangling at his side and drew forth the scintillant red emerald he had obtained from the bloated idol. Raising it toward the sun he said, "We shall do well with bauble, eh!"

Carthena gaped at the gem gasping in a terrified manner "The eye of Argon, Oh! Kalla!" At this the gem gave off a blinding glow, then dribbled through Grignr's fingers in a slimy red ooze. Grignr stepped back, pushing Carthena behind him. The droplets of slime slowly converged into a pulsating jelly-like mass. A single opening transfixed the blob, forminf into a leechlike maw.

Then the hideous transgressor of nature flowed towards Grignr, a trail of greenish slime lingering behind it. The single gap puckered repeatedly emitting a ghastly sucking sound.

Grignr spread his legs into a battle stance, steeling his quivering thews for a battle royal with a thing he knew not how to fight. Carthena wound her arms about her protectors neck, mumbling, "Kill it! Kill!" While her entire body trembled.

The thing was almost upon Grignr when he buried his axe into the gristly maw. It passed through the blob and clanged upon the ground. Grignr drew his axe back with a film of yellow-green slime clinging to the blade. The thing was seemingly unaffected. Then it started to slooze up his leg. The hairs upon his nape stoode on end from the slimey feel of the things buly, bulk. The Nautous sucking sound became louder, and Grignr felt the blood being drawn from his body. With each hiss of hideous pucker the thing increased in size.

Grignr shook his foot about madly in an attempt to dislodge the blob, but it clung like a leech, still feeding upon his rapidly draining life fluid. He grasped with his hands trying to rip it off, but only found his hands entangled in a sickly gluelike substance. The slimey thing continued its puckering ; now having grown the size of Grignr's leg from its vampiric feast.

Grignr began to reel and stagger under the blob, his chalk white face and faltering muscles attesting to the gigantic loss of blood. Carthena slipped from Grignr in a death-like faint, a morrow chilling scream upon her red rubish lips. In final desperation Grignr grasped the smoldering torch upon the ground and plunged it into the reeking maw of the travesty. A shudder passed through the thing. Grignr felt the blackness closing upon his eyes, but held on with the last ebb of his rapidly waning vitality. He could feel its grip lessoning as a hideous gurgling sound erupted from the writhing maw. The jelly like mass began to bubble like a vat of boiling tar as quavers passed up and down its entire form.

With a sloshing plop the thing fell to the ground, evaporating in a thick scarlet cloud until it reatained its original size. It remained thus for a moment as the puck-ered maw took the shape of a protruding red eyeball, the pupil of which seemed to unravel before it the tale of creation. How a shapeless mass slithered from the quag-mires of the stygmatic pool of time, only to degenerate into a leprosy of avaricious lust. In that fleeting moment the grim mystery of life was revealed before Grignr's ensnared gaze.

The eyeballs glare turned to a sudden plea of mercy, a plea for the whole of humanity. Then the blob began to quiver with violent convulsions; the eyeball shattered into a thousand tiny fragments and evaporated in a curling wisp of scarlet mist. The very ground below the thing began to vibrate and swallow it up with a belch.

The thing was gone forever. All that remained was a dark red blotch upon the face of the earth, blotching things up. Shaking his head, his shaggy mane to clear the jumbled fragments of his mind, Grignr tossed the limp female over his shoulder. Mounting one of the disgrun-tled mares, and leading the other; the weary, scarred barbarian trooted slowly off into the horizon to become a tiny pinpoint in a filtered filed of swirling blue mists, leaving the Nobles, soldiers and peasants to replace the missing monarch. Long leave the king!!!

By Jim Theis
winner of the Jay T. Rikosh award for excellence.